Jess the Goth Fairy

Jess Hiles & **Jo Allmond**

Illustrated by Emily Daly

Published in 2014 by the author
using SilverWood Books Empowered Publishing®

SilverWood Books Ltd
30 Queen Charlotte Street, Bristol, BS1 4HJ
www.silverwoodbooks.co.uk

ISBN 978-1-78132-203-1 (paperback)
ISBN 978-1-78132-269-7 (ebook)

British Library Cataloguing in Publication Data
A CIP catalogue record for this book is available from the British Library

Set in Sabon by SilverWood Books
Printed on responsibly sourced paper

SilverWood

For my best friend Helen
Jess xxx

My wonderful son Tom, Cath and beautiful grandson Sebastian
Jess without you there would be no book, no sunshine in my life.
Jo xxx

Jess loved to sit looking out of her home in the treetops first thing in the morning. Every day was different. As the sun said *hello* to the trees their leaves twinkled in its glow. She especially liked to watch the billowing clouds float out of the four tall things that she could never remember the name of. She watched them go high into the sky, higher than she could fly.

Jess was good at forgetting things. It came with her disability. Most of the time she didn't mind but occasionally she got upset, especially when some creatures laughed at her or were unkind. But her mum and dad told her she was special and that others were simply envious of all she could do.

"I'm off now, Mum," she shouted to her mother, who was inside the treetop home.

"Careful, Jess. Go straight to school. No talking to strangers," her mum called.

"Ok, Mum!" Jess called back.

"Promise?"

"I promise!" Jess shouted. With a wobble and a bang into a nearby branch, she flew off. Trying to fly smoothly was hard for Jess, as she was born with wings that were not the same size. They didn't work quite as well as other fairies' wings. But this did not stop Jess from trying to be normal, although at times this was hard. Some of the other fairies thought she should not be allowed to live as they did, which hurt Jess deeply.

As she flew, enjoying the feel of the gentle air on her face, something caught Jess's eye. She looked down and saw a group of birds who seemed to be making a lot of noise. One particularly large black and white bird she didn't recognise was being really nasty. Jess flew down a little closer and saw that in the middle of the group was a little bird being pushed around by the others.

That's Helen! Jess thought, recognising her best friend. Without hesitating, Jess started to fly down to help. Jess was not the best at flying, but landing was something she found even harder. Her lop-sided wings made her spin and tumble. Her feet were very small and an awkward shape, which made balancing difficult. Down…down…down she went.

"Ouch!" Jess landed with a bump on top of Helen, scattering the other birds away.

"Sorry, Helen." Jess said.

"Oh Jess, I wish you would learn to land properly," Helen said as she struggled to stand up.

"At least I got rid of those birds," Jess said. "What were they doing?"

"The same old thing. Because of my stupid tail they think it's fun to make me wobble by barging into me – especially if I am trying to get a drink. Being a long-tailed tit without a tail is not much fun!"

"I haven't seen that big black and white bird before," Jess said.

"Me neither, but it really seems to find me a big joke." Helen sighed.

"Well, they've gone now so let's get going. Can you give me a shove up with your beak?" Jess asked.

Helen put her beak under Jess's bottom and gave a big push, nearly falling over at the same time. Then they took off, narrowly missing crashing into each other.

After they had flown for a while they heard a screeching.

"What's that terrible noise?" Helen looked at Jess.

"I don't know," Jess replied. "It sounds as if someone's in pain or trouble."

They looked around, then Jess pointed to beyond the trees where the farmer's field started. There was a hedge very near to a wire fence, and a black and white bird seemed to be struggling and crying for help. The friends started to fly towards it.

"It's that bird – the one that's been bullying me. I'm not going down there," said Helen. She landed on a nearby branch.

Jess kept flying. "Come on, Helen, it seems to be caught and hurt."

"Serves it right. Hey, wait for me!"

They flew down, steadying one another as they got closer, then crash-landed on a bush near to where the bird was struggling. They saw that it was caught in a piece of wire that was sticking out of the fence into the hedge. The more the bird wriggled, the tighter the wire got.

"I would stop moving if I were you," Jess said.

The bird stopped wriggling and turned its head to where the voice was coming from.

"What would you know?" The bird squawked.

"I think you're making your leg more tangled. We've come to help," said Jess.

"What can *you* do? *You* can't fly properly and *she*," glaring at Helen, "can't move without wobbling or falling over."

"I told you that bird was horrible. I am not going to help it." Helen hopped higher up the bush.

"Stop it, the pair of you." Jess said, turning to the bird. "That is not a very nice thing to say about us. We may not look the same as others and perhaps we can't do things as well but we can try and help you. There is nobody else here." Jess looked at the bird, who was getting tired. "What's your name?" Jess asked.

"Anita," the bird said quietly.

"Well, Anita, I'm going to find a friend of mine who I think might be able to help." She turned to Helen, "Helen, you stay here and talk to Anita. Try to stop her wriggling any more."

"Why have I got to stay with her after all that she's done?" Helen argued.

"Do you know where to find Rich?" Jess asked.

"No." Helen sighed.

"Who's Rich?" asked Anita.

"A friend who can help, I hope. Helen will tell you all about him."

With that, Jess flew off, knocking into the hedge and bouncing into the air. "I'll be back as soon as I can."

Rich was searching for some breakfast. Stag beetles love old stale fruit, the older the better. The trouble was, Rich's eyesight was bad so it was hit or miss whether he could find some. When he did, it often turned out not to be what he thought it was!

"Rich! Rich!" Jess called, but Rich just carried on. He didn't like to be disturbed when he was food hunting.

"Rich, there you are," Jess said, landing just in front of him. "That wasn't a bad landing, if I say so myself!" she said, picking a piece of grass out of her ear.

"Uh, what, uh!" Rich was not a stag beetle of many words.

"Please, Rich, come with me. There's a bird in trouble and I think you can help," Jess said.

"Got to have my breakfast," grunted Rich.

"Please. It's urgent! I promise I'll help you find some juicy old apples if you do. I know where there are some good ones." Jess knew apples were Rich's favourites.

Rich stopped, thought for a minute, and grunted. Jess took this to mean "OK," so she jumped on his back and steered his pincers in the right direction.

When they got back, Anita was looking very tired. Although she did not seem to be bleeding, Jess could tell that she was in pain. Rich set about trying to cut through the wire with his pincers. Helen helped with her beak and Jess held Anita's leg. Eventually they managed to free her. Helen pulled up a big dock leaf and Jess wrapped this round Anita's leg, as it was looking a bit sore.

"Rich, you're a star. I knew you could do it!" Jess cried.

"Uh, what? OK, yep!" Rich replied and turned to go.

"Go down this lane and turn left," Jess said, tapping his left pincer. "You'll find loads of apples that have fallen off the trees already."

Rich was off.

"Thank you, Rich!" Anita shouted.

Jess turned to look at Anita, who was looking very shamefaced.

"Thank you and I'm sorry," Anita said.

"Sorry?" Helen and Jess looked at each other.

"Yes, sorry for all those things I said. It wasn't very kind of me, was it?"

"Not really, but we're used to it," Jess replied.

"Without you I could have been here for ages," Anita said.

"A fox might have got you," Helen butted in.

"Helen!" Jess glared at her.

"Sorry," Helen muttered.

Anita shook her head. "No, I deserved it."

"We only wanted to help," said Jess. "People think because we are disabled we can't do things, but we can."

"I know that now," said Anita, nodding her head.

"Sometimes it's hard being disabled," Jess went on. "We're seen as different – and we are in lots of ways. We look different and sometimes our bodies don't work like other creature's. And our brains can be slower, but inside we are the same as everyone else. We have feelings, and we get hurt when others can't see this. We want to be treated the same way, so we can all live together, help each other and be happy together." Jess looked at Anita.

"You have done more for me than I have ever done for anybody," Anita said. "I promise from now on I will try to help others, and not bully or tease." She glanced at Helen, who smiled back. "If I see someone being hurt, I will try to help them."

Anita put a wing round her two new friends. She gently helped them up into the air and waved them off.

"That was good, wasn't it, Helen? We have changed someone's attitude towards disability today." said Jess as they flew.

"I suppose we did!" said Helen with a smile.

"Oh come on," said Jess. "Race you to school!"

A Note From Jess

"I hope you enjoy my book. I had fun making it with mum. I hope it helps people to know what it is like to be like me and my friends. I am looking forward to going out and reading my story. I want to thank people who helped me."

Jess Hles

Thank You

Many thanks are due to Nadia Verdiani for the big push to get me going and endless support; Ed Hancox for his patience and advice; SilverWood Books for their belief, support and expertise; Emily Daly for bringing Jess to life with her talent and finally, Alan Allmond for being there with the tissues and cups of tea.

We'd also like to thank our Kickstarter backers. Without you all there would be no book. Your support and generosity has been overwhelming! We wish to give a special mention to the following backers who have made sure Jess the Goth Fairy will spread her wings: MacIntyre, Andrew, Sian Smith and family, Richard Farmer, Rosa Monckton and lastly, Kickstarter for the opportunity to fulfil a dream.

A donation from sales of this book will be made to MacIntyre (macintyrecharity.org).

About the Authors

Jess, who is the inspiration for this book, although having learning and physical disabilities, lives independently in Worcestershire with support. She has achieved so much – she is a National Special Olympic gold and silver medallist, has become a member of the Peoples Parliament of Worcestershire for the disabled, helps teach sign language at a day centre and also works in a garden nursery. Jess wants nothing more than to help others, especially those less able than herself. She hopes by sharing her feelings in this book it will help everyone to know what it is like to be disabled.

Jo lives in Shropshire where she now designs and makes crafts, but her career began as a ballet dancer having been privileged to dance with Fonteyn and Nureyev. Injury brought her dancing career to an early close, so she taught creative dance in mainstream schools and for 15 years ran a theatre company for able/disabled young people; this being started to help Jess and others have fun and a social life in the community. Jo's biggest achievements in her life are her children, Tom and Jess.

Lightning Source UK Ltd.
Milton Keynes UK
UKIC01n1218201014
240292UK00011B/64

9 781781 322031